W9-CBS-595

Big Bird's Square Meal

Stories About Shapes and Colors

By Emily Thompson
Illustrated by Tom Brannon

A Sesame Street/Golden Press Book

Published by Western Publishing Company, Inc., in conjunction
with Children's Television Workshop.

Big Bird's Square Meal

"Oh, my little Big Bird!" said Granny Bird as she arrived at Big Bird's nest. "How you've grown!"

"Thanks, Granny," said Big Bird. "I can't wait for our picnic."

"Come, then, dear," said Granny. "Cookie Monster and Elmo are waiting outside."

"What's in your basket, Granny?" asked Big Bird as they settled on a green grassy spot next to the duck pond.

"I've packed a good square meal for us!" said Granny.

"I know what a square is!" said Elmo proudly. "And I know all about circles and rectangles and triangles, too! Maria is helping me learn my shapes."

"Okay, Elmo," said Big Bird as he helped Granny unpack the picnic basket. "What shape is this tablecloth?"

"A rectangle!" said Elmo.

"Right, Elmo," said Granny. "But look what happens when I help Big Bird unfold it."

"Now it's a square," said Elmo, "with little red-and-white squares all over it."

"Time for PICNIC!" cried Cookie Monster.

"Here are some peanut-butter-and-jelly sandwiches," said Granny.

"Look! More squares!" said Elmo.

Cookie Monster couldn't take it anymore. "Give me square!" he yelled as he bit into a sandwich.

"Now all that's left of the square sandwich is a triangle," said Big Bird.

"Who knows what shape this is?" asked Granny,
holding up a piece of watermelon.

"It looks like a squashed circle," said Big Bird.

"It's not a circle," said Elmo. "This pie is a circle.
See? It's round."

"Give me circle!" yelled Cookie.

"This watermelon piece is an oval," said Elmo.

"Give me oval!" said Cookie as he gobbled up the watermelon.

"Now, here's an important shape," said Elmo, holding up his milk carton. "It's called a pentagon."
"Give me pentagon!" said Cookie as he gobbled down the milk, carton and all. "Cowabunga!"

"Now it's not a pentagon," said Big Bird. "It's just gone like the rest of our picnic.

"What's in your bag, Cookie Monster?" asked Big Bird.

"More shapes!" said Elmo.
"Not shapes," said Cookie Monster, "COOOKIES!"

"COWABUNGA!" his friends cried. "He's right!"
And they gobbled up the rectangles and squares and
triangles and circles and ovals and pentagons.

Who Ever Heard of
a Purple Puppy?

Saturday morning, when Ernie and Bert woke up,
it was raining.

"What shall we do today?" asked Bert.

"I know," said Ernie, "let's color!"

Bert got down his crayons and Ernie pulled out
some paper. They both worked hard on their pictures.

"All done," said Bert.

"What did you draw, Bert?" asked Ernie. Bert proudly held up his picture of a gray pigeon sitting in a green tree against a bright blue sky.

"Let's see yours," said Bert.

Ernie held up his picture.

"It's a nice picture, Ernie," said Bert, "but you made the sky pink! Sky isn't pink, it's blue. Trees aren't yellow. They're green like the tree in my picture. And who ever heard of a purple puppy?"

"Just use your imagination, Bert," said Ernie.

"Oh, sure, Ernie," said Bert. "I can see that I need to teach you about colors."

Just then the sun peeked out, and the sky turned a brilliant blue. Ernie and Bert raced outside.

"See, Ernie, the sky is blue," said Bert. "And here is Grover. He is blue, too."

"Oh, I am not blue," said Grover. "I am happy because my grandmonster sent me this cute and adorable blue jean jacket."

"No, no, Grover," said Bert. "I didn't mean that you felt blue. I meant that the color of your fur is blue."

"That is true," said Grover. "Would you like a blueberry?"

"Cowabunga!" said another blue monster. "Someone say blueberry?"

RRRrrreee-OOOooowww! screamed the siren of a red fire engine as it roared past. Everyone turned to watch, including Elmo, who was carrying a bag of groceries home from the store. He walked right into a fire hydrant and dropped the groceries—SPLAT— onto the sidewalk. Ernie and Bert ran to help.

"Oh, look," said Bert. "These apples and tomatoes are another important color. They're red, just like that fire engine."

"Elmo's red, too," said Ernie.

"Right, old buddy," said Bert. "You're catching on."

"Taxi! Oh, taxi, yoo-hoooo!" yelled Big Bird from the corner.

"Where are you going, Big Bird?" asked Ernie.

"I'm taking these flowers to Granny Bird for her birthday," said Big Bird.

"Never mind that, Ernie," said Bert. "Look, this is great! Notice Big Bird—a big yellow bird—holding yellow daffodils, getting into a yellow cab. Now, that makes a beautiful picture."

"Thank you," said Big Bird. "Good-bye!"

"Now, let's see," said Bert. "I've taught you about
blue, red, and yellow. What can I show you that's
orange?"

"I don't know, Bert," said Ernie as he bought a
piece of fruit at Mr. McIntosh's fruit stand. "Want a
piece?"

"Oh, sure, thanks," said Bert. "I'd love a section of
your...ORANGE! Ernie, your orange is the color
orange!"

"Gee, Bert," said Ernie. "Orange you glad I bought
an orange? Hee, hee, hee!"

As Ernie and Bert walked by Oscar's trash can,
they heard a terrible crashing and clanging of lids.
"Oh, yeah?" grouched Oscar.
"Yeah!" yelled Grungetta.
"Says who?" asked Oscar.
"Says me!" screamed Grungetta.

"Uh, excuse me," said Bert.

"WHAT DO YOU WANT?" yelled Oscar and Grungetta.

"I just wanted to show Ernie something green, and you two are perfect examples. See, Ernie—Oscar and Grungetta are green like leaves on a tree, or grass, or vegetables like broccoli, green beans, peas…"

"Hey," said Oscar. "Who are you calling perfect?"

"Yeah," said Grungetta. "Who?"

"We'll just be going now," said Ernie.

CRASH! The two trash can lids slammed shut.

Then Ernie and Bert heard a crash coming from the arbor area. They walked over to investigate.

"Don't worry," said Prairie Dawn. "I just knocked over our sign."

"Here, let me help you," said Bert as he picked up the sign from the sidewalk. "Frosty Fruit Fizzies. Ten cents," he read.

"That's right," said Prairie. "Telly and I are going
into business. What flavor would you like: grape,
lime, orange, lemon, cherry, or blueberry?"

"I'll take one grape, please," said Bert. Prairie
Dawn poured him a tall cup of juice, and Bert handed
over a dime. "Now, here's another neat color, Ernie.
Grape juice is purple like grapes, or eggplants, or
violets."

Just then Barkley and some of his puppy friends
dashed around the corner, chasing a ball. "See?" Bert
told Ernie. "Puppies can be white, or black, or brown,
or sometimes all three. But they are never purple."

The ball rolled right between Bert's feet. The little
white puppy dived after it, knocking the cup from
Bert's hand. Grape juice splashed all over the puppy.

"Look, Bert," said Ernie, laughing. "A purple puppy!"

"Now I've seen everything!" said Bert.